For Missy

PUFFIN BOOKS

UK | USA | Canada | Ireland | Australia | India | New Zealand | South Africa

Puffin Books is part of the Penguin Random House group of companies
whose addresses can be found at global.penguinrandomhouse.com.

www.penguin.co.uk   www.puffin.co.uk   www.ladybird.co.uk

Penguin
Random House
UK

First published 2019
001

Text and illustrations copyright © Sophy Henn, 2019
The moral right of the author/illustrator has been asserted
Printed and bound in China
A CIP catalogue record for this book is available from the British Library
Hardback ISBN: 978–0–141–37075–0
Paperback ISBN: 978–0–141–38548–8
All correspondence to: Puffin Books, Penguin Random House Children's
80 Strand, London WC2R 0RL

MIX
Paper from
responsible sources
FSC® C018179

SUPER DUPER YOU

Sophy Henn

PUFFIN

I've known you
since you started.
I've seen a thing
or two . . .

. . . or three, or four,

or five, or six!

In fact, I've seen a few!

To do...
Have fun

And something that I've spotted
while I've watched you grow and grow
is that you're lots of different things,
more than you could know!

Sometimes you're this,
sometimes you're that . . .

Sometimes you're in between!
It's hard to say what makes you, YOU.
I'll show you what I mean . . .

Sometimes you are all twinkly,
with frills and jewels and bows.
You waft and float about the place,
all twirls and tippy-toes.

And sometimes you are clanky,
all fighty, bold and brave.
You stomp about and shout out loud
and look for things to save.

Sometimes you're a bad baddie,
thinking bad baddie thoughts.

Then suddenly you're super,

with pants outside your shorts!

Sometimes when you're cuddly
you're a flopsy cutie pie,
full of smiles and love and hugs,
a real-life lullaby.

You're sometimes super silly,
the funniest I've known!

And sometimes very quiet,
in a world all of
your own.

Sometimes you're polka-dotty

when everyone's in stripes.

Sometimes you don't know
what you are . . .

and nothing is
quite right.

But those things that make you different
are the things that make you, YOU!
Without those things you're someone else,
and that would never do!

The trick is not to worry
about what you are not.
Instead enjoy the things you are
and all the brills you've got!

Yes, you're so many different things . . .

You'll be so many more.

There really is no limit
to what you have in store.

But please try to remember,
with everything you do . . .

be bold,

be **proud**,

be **brilliant** . . .

A
SUPER
DUPER
YOU!